AGAIN RAGS

Rags, Tatters and Binks

AGAIN RAGS

By

LEWIS DUTTON

Illustrated by

EDGAR NORFIELD

jD954a

FREDERICK WARNE AND CO., LTD.
LONDON
FREDERICK WARNE AND CO., INC.
NEW YORK

PRINTED IN GREAT BRITAIN

To ZULU—

A WEE ABERDEEN TERRIER WITH A HEART
OF GOLD—I INSCRIBE THIS STORY OF
MR. BINKS AND HIS THREE TRUSTY
FRIENDS, RAGS, TATTERS
AND BILL

CONTENTS

AGAIN
RAGS

RAGS SLOWLY BACKED OUT

A FAMOUS VICTORY

"MICHAEL'S going shopping!" announced Tatters, bursting into the nursery.

Rags, who was busy inside the toy cupboard, slowly backed out. Now it was not Rags' usual custom to walk backwards, but at the moment he had Michael's kite gripped across his jaws, and though the doorway had been wide enough to admit him when he went

9

into the cupboard alone, it seemed to have grown strangely narrow when he tried to come out in company with a large red kite. However, with a little backward manœuvring, in which his tail appeared first, then the rest of his body attached to the kite, the whole of Rags was once again visible.

" Well, why don't you say something? " snapped Tatters, who didn't like his news being received in silence.

" You—you can't—say something with a—a—mouth full of kite! " panted Rags.

" Then why don't you drop it? "

" You—you can't—drop it," came the desperate reply. "At least, not when it's stuck to you! "

Rags struggled—there was a rip—then his head burst through the red cover.

"Now you've torn it! " squealed Tatters.

10

Rags knew he'd torn it, for how could his head be one side of the kite and his tail the other unless there was a hole somewhere?

"It doesn't matter," he said airily. "Michael doesn't use it in the winter, so there's lots of time to find him another before he wants it again —p'raps we'll see one to-day when we go shopping."

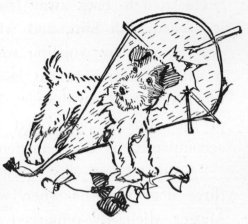

RAGS KNEW HE'D TORN IT

"Bill!" came a shout from Michael in the hall below; and the Airedale, who was lazily stretched before the nursery fire, sprang up and obediently trotted downstairs. Tatters

11

followed, leaving Rags still tied up in the kite.

" Rags! " Michael again called.

" Bother! " spluttered Rags.

He tried to back away from the kite, but it backed with him, and when he tried to get rid of it by whirling round and round, it whirled with him. At last, giving up the unequal struggle in despair, Rags dashed out of the nursery and rolled downstairs, still accompanied by the persistent kite.

" I don't know why we must always take three dogs with us when we go shopping, Master Michael," remarked Jane. " I don't mind Bill, he's old enough to know how to behave, but what with a car full of parcels and puppies——"

" The car won't be full of puppies, Jane," said Michael. " Rags and Tatters are only two."

"Yes; and they make as much noise as twenty-two," said Jane tartly. "What with yapping and—— My goodness—what's that!"

She turned a shocked glance at the staircase down which there came rolling and sliding a confused bunch of ears, legs, and kite tightly locked together; at one moment Rags was on top; then the kite got the upper hand, until at last, still clinging together, they landed with a bump on the mat at the foot of the stairs.

THEY LANDED WITH A BUMP

13

" Oh, Rags, you are naughty! " cried Michael, as he parted the breathless culprit from the battered remains of the kite.

Rags hurriedly thrust an apologetic nose into Michael's hand, and tried to tell him that a new kite would be found at the very first opportunity.

But Jane bundled them into the car, and Rags was afraid Michael hadn't understood, so he curled himself up on the seat and tried to look as penitent as a small dog ought to look when he has deliberately smashed up a perfectly good kite; and he softly whimpered now and again just to tell himself how really sorry he was feeling, until he suddenly found that Jane's bag was within reach of his teeth, and after quietly chewing a hole in it, he felt so comforted that when the car drew up before one of the big shops, he was quite ready to join brother Tatters in hurling a ferocious challenge at the large gold - braided gentleman who was guarding the entrance.

"Now, Bill, take care of Rags and Tatters," said Michael, when he and Jane got out of the car, and shut the dogs inside.

"No chance of getting a kite now," grumbled

THE LARGE GOLD-BRAIDED GENTLEMAN

15

Rags. " I do think Jane might have taken us into the shop."

" Yes, we'd have been ever so good," said Tatters. " At least, I *think* we would," he added doubtfully.

At this moment the large gold-braided gentleman hurried across the pavement and opened the door of the car.

" That isn't my car," said a lady, who had just come out of the shop, " the next one."

The large gold-braided gentleman apologised, and turned away from Michael's car, leaving the door still open.

" Come on, Tatters! " cried Rags, springing out; and in a twinkling the pair had streaked into the shop.

Bill followed, for Michael's order had been, " take care of Rags and Tatters." When he arrived in the shop, however, the puppies had vanished, so he quietly padded up the wide staircase on a voyage of discovery.

Meanwhile, Rags and Tatters had come to a halt near the open door of a small room.

" Wonder if the kites are in there? " Rags peered inside; but at that moment the door shut with a clang, and the little room flew away.

" Yes, the kites must have been in there," cried Tatters. " They've flown away with the room itself! "

In a few moments, however, the little room came sliding down, and when the door opened the puppies entered.

" Hello, what do you two want? " said the boy who had charge of the little room.

A rapid wagging of two stubby tails intimated that a kite was urgently needed; but the boy only grinned, and the room

17

having now filled with people, he shut the door and again sailed upwards.

"It's all feet in here, isn't it, Rags?" whispered Tatters, shrinking into a corner.

But when the little room had flown as high as it could go, the feet all got out.

"IT'S ALL FEET IN HERE"

"Well, ain't you pups got nobody belongin' to yer?" enquired the lift-boy, as Rags and Tatters remained behind.

Two stubby tails again wagged the information that Rags and Tatters had lots

18

of quite important people belonging to them, but they didn't intend to budge until a kite had been produced, so down again went the little room and its occupants.

For the next ten minutes Rags and Tatters spent their time in going up and down in the lift, until at last, when it ended one journey at the top, they saw Bill.

" There's Bill! " squealed Tatters; and they flung themselves on their big pal joyously, telling him all about their journey in the funny little kite room, " which made you feel as if your tummy was where it wasn't," as Rags said.

" But the kites are in here," said Bill. " I've just seen lots of them," and nosing open the swing doors of a huge room filled with toys, he led the puppies inside.

Bill was right, but kites weren't the only

things they found in the toy room—Michael
and Jane were also there.

" We'd better go back to the car," said
Bill hurriedly. " Michael didn't want us to
follow him."

The trio turned to retreat, but suddenly
found themselves confronted by dozens of
dogs—in fact, one corner of the toy room,
that they hadn't noticed when they entered,
seemed to be filled with dogs of every breed.
Tatters pressed close to Bill for protection,
but Rags stiffened.

" Come on, Tatters," he said boldly, " let's
fight 'em."

" What, the whole lot? " shivered Tatters.

" Yes, we'll start with that chap in the
front—he seems to be the leader of the pack."

Rags stalked towards his adversary; Tatters
followed reluctantly.

" Good afternoon," said Rags, addressing the leader.

The only reply he got was a glassy stare.

" Impudent cur! " muttered Tatters, gaining courage by the silence. " I don't like the look of him."

" Neither do I," Rags agreed. " Let's teach him good manners."

"Let's teach the whole lot! " exclaimed Tatters valiantly.

PRICES FROM 10/6 TO 21/-

"IMPUDENT CUR!" MUTTERED TATTERS

21

" G'rrrrr! " snarled Rags, and leapt at the silent leader.

" G'rrrrr! " echoed Tatters, and flung himself into the middle of the equally silent pack. " Come on, Bill—you help."

Bill was too honourable to fight dogs smaller than himself, but at the other end of the room he saw a large yellow animal lurking near a doll's house, and he padded towards it eagerly. When he was within a few paces, however, he stopped, for he saw that the animal was a large yellow tiger just crouching for a spring, and right in front of it stood Michael, absorbed in choosing a new kite. There wasn't a moment to be lost. Gathering himself together, Bill took a flying leap on to the tiger's back, and they crashed over together.

" You cowardly brute, sneaking up to Michael like that—I'll teach you!" Bill's

22

"No fight in 'em!" said Rags

teeth pressed deep into the tiger's neck, and tore a hole in the yellow skin; something soft and woolly tickled Bill's nose.

" Pooh! " he snorted. " You're only stuffed, after all, and I thought you were real! " and with a disgusted sniff at the flattened tiger, Bill trotted away to see how Rags and Tatters were getting on with their own particular bit of havoc.

The puppies had lost no time in routing the enemy; the leader was already flat on his back gazing at the ceiling with the same glassy stare, and around him lay the mangled remains of the pack.

" No fight in 'em! " said Rags, stopping to breathe.

" No—awful limp crowd! " Tatters picked up a Pom by its middle, gave the furry body a good shake, and tossed it away.

23

"Wuff! Wuff!" yelped Rags, just to let the world know what a couple of brave pups they were.

But his triumph was short-lived, **for** the next moment he and Tatters were seized by the scruff of the neck.

THE PUPPIES HAD LOST NO TIME

"Who owns these pups?"

Somebody held the culprits aloft so that they could be claimed at once. But nobody wanted to claim them—in fact, everybody hastily assured everybody else that they had no connection whatever with the disgraceful couple.

" Bill! " squealed Tatters, struggling to get free. " Come and rescue us! "

Bill heard the S O S and leapt to answer it, but when he reached the puppies, he found that Michael and Jane had already arrived on the scene.

" Take Rags and Tatters away, Master Michael, while I see what damage they have done," said Jane severely; and gathering the pair of rascals into his arms, Michael departed, followed by Bill, whose drooping head showed that he was suffering from a very bad pain in his conscience.

News of the exploit spread quickly—the lift-boy confided to the messenger-boy that " them two pups ain't 'arf smashed up the toy department, they 'aven't . . . thought

25

them toy dogs was real, an' started in to worry 'em!'' and the messenger-boy gave a joyous " Whoop!" and slid down the bannisters to hand on the news to the large gold-braided gentleman, who, in turn, remarked to Michael's chauffeur, Hopkins, " Nearly wrecked our toy department, those two puppies of yours—followed your young gent inside, they did."

" Yes, they're a fine spirited pair," replied Hopkins proudly. " Can't think what Master Michael would do without 'em—follows him about everywhere, just like his shadder, they do."

" H'm!" growled the gold-braided gentleman; and putting Michael and his " shadder " inside the car, he firmly shut the door on them until Jane appeared, and they all drove home.

II

RAGS had a secret; for a whole week he trotted about the house looking very superior, and occasionally he dropped mysterious hints about somebody called "Slinker."

"Wonder if Slinker does much ratting?" he would murmur, as though talking to himself, or —"I must take Slinker to the Round Pond and introduce him to our lot down there." But whenever Tatters asked, "Who is Slinker?" Rags always remembered something that required his immediate attention, and he was deaf to the question.

27

" Wonder what Slinker is having to-day? " he remarked one dinner-time, when he and Tatters were nosing about their dish for the graviest bits of biscuit. " Of course, a dog like Slinker wouldn't dream of—of——"

Rags stopped eating to consider just *what* the unknown Slinker " wouldn't dream of," and Tatters took quick advantage of the pause to gobble up his brother's portion as well as his own. After this, Rags took care not to mention Slinker at meal times.

One morning, however, when Rags, Tatters and Bill had returned from their walk in Kensington Gardens, where Rags had been unusually boastful about " my friend, Slinker," Tatters decided that something drastic had got to be done in the matter, and he made up his mind to take the very first chance that offered. He hadn't long to wait.

" Thought of inviting Slinker to go with us this morning," Rags began in a casual tone, when they were lazing on the nursery hearthrug.

" Where's Bill? " asked Tatters.

"LET GO!" SQUEALED RAGS

" Gone to help Jane take off Michael's shoes," replied Rags shortly. He was rather offended at Tatters' lack of interest in his remark.

Hearing that Bill was safely out of the way, Tatters edged a bit nearer to the unsuspecting

Rags, who had now returned to his all-absorbing subject.

"You see, I thought p'raps Slinker might——"

But Tatters pounced, and his teeth closed with a snap on his brother's tail.

"Let go!" squealed Rags, struggling to free himself.

"Not until you've told me who Slinker is," mumbled Tatters, holding on tight.

"I'll tell you if you'll leave my tail alone," promised Rags.

Tatters' grip loosened; and after giving an anxious wag to the assaulted tail, to see if it was still safely attached to his person, Rags began:

"You know that little room at the top of the house?"

"Yes—Jane calls it the box room."

"Well, she went up there one day to look

for something in Michael's big trunk, and I
went with her just——"

"Just in case she was looking for a bone,"

Tatters prompt-
ed helpfully.
"Yes."
"Did she find one?"

"I WENT WITH HER" "No; but while she
was busy, I sniffed about to see if I could
find a bit of chocolate or—or——"

31

" Or a biscuit."

" Yes."

" Did you find one? " Tatters was dreadfully inquisitive this morning.

" No; but I found something else," Rags looked mysterious.

" Go on," urged Tatters impatiently. " What was it? "

" A grey dog! "

" Wh-where was it? " Tatters shivered with excitement.

" Lurking just behind me. I didn't see it at first, but I suddenly sensed danger, so I sprang round quickly to protect Jane, and there was the dog standing close to the wall."

" Did it growl? "

" No, not even when *I* growled, and it slinked away when I followed Jane out of the box room—that's why I call it ' Slinker '."

" Does it live in the box room? "

" I think so, but I have seen it lurking near me in other parts of the house sometimes." Rags was rather pleased to think that the grey dog had picked him out as a special object of attention. " Of course, if I see it anywhere near Michael, I'll soon send it packing back to its box room—I'm not going to have any Slinker prowling about near him."

" But it doesn't have its dinner with us," said Tatters.

" No, I don't think Slinker ever has dinner —he looks awful thin."

Tatters was troubled. To live in a box room and not to have any dinner was such a dreadful fate that poor Slinker must be rescued from it at once.

" We'll give him half our dinner—the largest

33

half," he said generously, " and we'll carry it up at night when nobody's about."

" Hush! " interrupted Rags. " Here's Bill, and we've got to keep Slinker a secret."

Later on that same day, when it was dusk, two small white forms crept upstairs to the box room, which had now been renamed " Slinker's kennel," and one had a meaty bone gripped between its teeth, while the other carried half a biscuit and a piece of sponge cake. The offerings were laid outside the door, and the next morning, when the same two forms again hurried up to Slinker's kennel, they found that every crumb had been eaten.

After this, it was a regular custom for Rags and Tatters stealthily to ascend the upper stairs with tit-bits for Slinker, and one night Tatters nobly added to the bountiful feast a squashed chocolate cream which was his own private property.

"Do you think Slinker likes chocolate creams?" he asked, later on, when he and Rags were curled up in their basket.

"Sure to," replied Rags.

Tatters sighed—it had been a tremendous sacrifice parting with that chocolate cream.

"Do you think I—we—might go up and give it one more lick before Slinker finds it?" he pleaded.

EVERY CRUMB HAD BEEN EATEN

Rags agreed, and in a moment the couple were scurrying up to Slinker's kennel.

"Listen!" Rags stopped at the corner

THEY PEEPED ROUND THE CORNER AND SAW—BILL!

of the little passage into which the moon was shining through a small skylight. In the silence they heard a soft "scrunch— scrunch"—Slinker was eating his supper.

36

" Let's peep round the corner and watch him," whispered Tatters. They crawled forward, peeped round the corner, and saw—Bill!

" Oh, Bill—how could you eat poor Slinker's supper! " they cried reproachfully.

" Slinker's supper? " Bill looked puzzled. " Who's Slinker? "

" My grey dog—I mean, he's mine and Tatters's," replied Rags, " and he lives in the box room."

Bill sniffed along the bottom of the closed door.

" I don't smell him," he said doubtfully.

" But he must be in there," insisted Rags, " because he comes out every night and eats the supper we leave here for him."

Bill looked guilty. " I—I thought Michael had put it here for me, just in case I felt hungry when I go round the house at night to see that all's safe."

Bill was dreadfully penitent when he found he had been enjoying a nightly supper that was meant for somebody else, and he instantly began to suggest plans for Slinker's comfort.

" He must have three good meals a day——"

" Yes, and scraps in between," added Tatters drowsily.

" And we'll put some soft cushions in his kennel," yawned Rags.

" Yes, *lots* of soft cush—sh—h—" Bill's head dropped on to his paws, and the only sound heard outside Slinker's kennel was a chorus of tuneful snores.

A CHORUS OF TUNEFUL SNORES

38

III

"MISTER BINKS"

MICHAEL was so excited that he could hardly eat his breakfast, for the postman had brought a letter to say that Grandfather was coming up to Town, and would take Michael back with him to spend Christmas at Merriemead.

"HOW DO GOOD BOYS EAT THEIR BREAKFAST, JANE?"

" Please, Jane——" began Michael.

" Now eat your breakfast like a good boy, Master Michael, and don't keep asking questions," said Jane.

39

" How *do* good boys eat their breakfast, Jane? " Michael's spoonful of porridge paused on its way to his mouth. " I mean, don't good boys and naughty boys eat in the same way? "

Jane glanced severely over the top of the coffee-pot, and Michael hurriedly swallowed the spoonful of porridge.

" Has Grandfather invited Rags and Tatters as well as me? " he asked, when his tongue was again free for polite conversation.

" No, of course he hasn't," replied Jane. " He doesn't want to be bothered with two such tiresome puppies."

But Jane was mistaken, for when Grandfather arrived Bill thrust a moist and friendly nose into his hand, and Rags and Tatters thoughtfully assisted him to eat his cake at

40

tea-time, and Grandfather was so pleased with their very warm welcome that he said they must all come down to Merriemead and spend Christmas with Binks.

The next morning the trio were up early, before the household was astir, for they had to carry out their plans for Slinker's comfort before starting off for Merriemead. Bill made several journeys up to the box room, and laid outside the door a good supply of dog biscuit, topped by a mouldy bone that he had dug up in Kensington Gardens the previous day; while Rags and Tatters bumped their way upstairs with the cushion out of their own basket, and laid it beside the pile of biscuits. Having thus provided for Slinker's comfort during their absence, they helped Michael to have his bath, and afterwards shepherded him to the breakfast table.

D*

41

When a few more good deeds of this
kind had been successfully carried out, Rags,
Tatters and Bill were just in the right trim

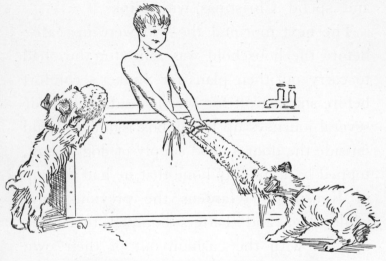

THEY HELPED MICHAEL TO HAVE HIS BATH

for an enjoyable Christmas holiday, and they
started off to Merriemead, taking with them
the highest of spirits and the best of
behaviour.

Except that Tatters ate Grandfather's ham sandwich out of the luncheon basket, quite by mistake, nothing very disturbing happened on the journey until they reached Merriemead, and the car swung into the long beech avenue, then they heard the sound of excited barking. Three pairs of ears were instantly cocked.

" It's Slinker! " cried Rags joyously. " He must have got out of the box room, and followed us all the way from Town."

" No, it isn't," said Bill. "It's Grandfather's dog, Binks."

" Is he very big and savage? " Tatters looked anxious.

" No, he isn't very big—he's an Aberdeen terrier, and Michael said he was very intelligent."

" What's 'telligent? " asked Rags.

43

"Well, it means that he knows how to obey orders," explained Bill. "If Grandfather puts his glove on the floor and tells Binks to guard it while he's away, Binks just lies near it quietly and won't let anybody touch it—he doesn't chew it up, and bury it in the garden like you would."

When the car stopped, and they all went into the house, Binks flung himself on Grandfather, and just to show how very pleased he was to see his master again, he joyously corkscrewed after his own tail until he accidentally rammed Bill, whom he had not yet noticed; in a flash his crest stiffened.

"It's all right, old chap," said Grandfather reassuringly; "these are three new pals for you to play with."

Binks, being so very 'telligent, understood at once, and after giving Bill a friendly

nuzzle, turned his attention to Rags and
Tatters.

"Hello, pups!" he said, in a condes-
cending tone.

"HELLO, PUPS!"
SAID BINKS

"Hello, Binks!" replied Rags jauntily.

"*Mister* Binks, if you please," responded
the Aberdeen gravely. For a moment he

45

gazed over Rags's head at nothing in particular, then continued, " I own Grandfather and Mister Timson."

" Who's Mister Timson? " asked Tatters.

" The butler."

" Well, *we* own Michael and Jane."

" Yes, and Slinker! " snapped Rags.

Binks stared in pained surprise at the scrap of canine impudence defying him, then turned away, and with a dignified trot, disappeared into one of the rooms opening out of the large square hall. In a few moments, however, he returned.

" Er—who's Slinker? " he asked in a casual tone.

Binks was just longing to know who the mysterious Slinker might be, but it wouldn't do to let these cheeky young pups see that he was interested.

Rags explained, and after giving a glowing description of Slinker's character, with a few extra qualities thrown in for Binks' special benefit, he ended:

" I'm afraid he'll be ever so lonely without us."

Binks took the hint. " You may bring him with you when next you come," he said graciously.

Nothing more was needed to cement the friendship; and when, in a further burst of hospitality, Binks offered to show his guests a few of the most interesting sights and smells of Merriemead, Rags, Tatters and Bill felt thoroughly at home in their new surroundings.

A stately procession of four, with Mister Binks at the head, crossed the hall and turned down a small passage ending in a green

47

baize door. Binks had long since discovered that he could easily open this door by hurling

his tough little body against it; but on the present occasion these acrobatics were not required, as Bill's nose, deftly inserted in the crack, was sufficient persuasion to swing the door open.

On the other side, the passage continued, and the

TATTERS VAN-
ISHED THROUGH
AN OPEN DOOR-
WAY

48

procession again formed into line; but Tatters, who brought up the rear suddenly paused, then quietly dropped out of the ranks and vanished through an open doorway from which came the appetising smell of cooking. A moment later Rags also paused, sniffed the air, then quietly vanished in the same direction.

" Now ain't they a puffect pair! " exclaimed Cook admiringly, as the puppies entered her kitchen; and dividing a mince pie, she presented a portion to each half of the " puffect pair."

Rags and Tatters at once decided that Cook was quite the most interesting sight in Merriemead, and that further exploring was merely a waste of time, so they remained in the kitchen.

Meanwhile, Binks had led Bill into the

garden and down to the potting-shed where, in his opinion, Merriemead's greatest treasures were stored; and he now proceeded to display them to his guest's admiring eyes.

" This," he explained, " is my stick."

Bill gripped the stick across his jaws to test its quality.

" It's got a good balance," he remarked in the tone of an expert.

Binks looked pleased, and turned to the next exhibit.

" This is my ball. Grandfather likes to throw it across the lawn, but I get a bit tired in bringing it back to him so often."

Binks yawned in a casual way, but there was an anxious gleam in his eye when he saw Bill nose the precious ball that belonged exclusively to Grandfather and himself.

As Bill turned to look at other treasures, he suddenly noticed a good-sized bone lying in one corner of the shed. He paused, and stared in fascinated silence.

Binks hurriedly tried to turn his attention to other objects, but Bill's eyes kept wandering back to the bone, so Binks brought it out of the corner, and laid it at Bill's feet.

" That's my new bone," he explained. " I was just going to bury it when you all arrived." He gave his treasure a sniff, then nosed it nearer to Bill. " I say," he exclaimed generously, " you may lick it if you likc, and I don't mind if you give it a good scrunch as well! "

But Bill was a gentleman, and when one gentleman trusts another gentleman with his bone it isn't honourable to give it a scrunch, so after one small lick he politely turned away.

51

" Thank you, Binks. It's a most superior bone—ham, I think? "

" Yes—very hammy," agreed Binks. " Of

"IT'S A MOST SUPERIOR BONE"

course, I wouldn't have trusted it to those two pups you've brought with you."

Bill shuddered to think just *what* Rags and Tatters would have done with that bone if they'd been allowed to give it even half a sniff; but he assured Binks that they were really very fine little chaps, and that Michael thought all the world of them.

" And now I'll show you my very best rat hole," said Binks, when sundry other treasures had been duly admired.

He crawled under a bench against which some garden tools were stacked. Bill followed, but found the space uncomfortably cramped for his long legs.

" It's just here," whispered Binks. " Keep quiet, and you'll hear the rats sneaking about under the floor—there are lots of 'em down there—great, big, savage brutes with awful sharp teeth—perfect crowd of 'em rush out sometimes."

" Catch many? " enquired Bill, with a grunt of satisfaction.

" H'm—well——" The fact was Binks had never seen even the tip of a rat's whisker in the potting shed, so he turned aside the question by suggesting—" S'pose we do a bit of hunting together while you're staying with us—eh? "

" Yes—rather! " exclaimed Bill.

" S'hush! " Binks edged nearer and gave a cautious sniff. " Those chaps down there are beginning to move about now. I can hear a wuffly-scuffly noise."

" Best way to catch 'em is just to blow 'em out," advised Bill.

" Blow them out? "

" Yes; they're sure to have a bolt hole leading outside, so if we blow hard this end, then dash out quick, we'll catch the whole lot as they scurry out the other end."

" Good! " cried Binks. " We'll blow together."

There was a united blow, the dust rose in a cloud, and for the next few minutes nothing was heard in the potting shed but

THE DUST ROSE IN A CLOUD

a duet of resounding sneezes. While it was in progress, Tim Stubbs, the gardener's boy, came in.

"Hello, Binks!" he cried. "What be makin' 'ee sneezle like that? Reckon 'ee bin nosin' down the mouse 'ole under the bench, but 'tain't no use, fer I stopped it up this mornin'."

Only a *mouse* hole, after all! Bill cast a reproachful glance at Binks, but that enthusiastic hunter had already dashed outside to see how many rats were scuttling away to safer quarters, so Bill wasn't sure if he had heard Tim's remark; and later on, when they went indoors again and Binks invited his three guests to share the hearthrug in front of the library fire, Bill was much too polite to mention rat—or rather, mouse holes.

IV

RAGS AND SANTA CLAUS

"JANE, do you think Santa Claus will really see it?" Michael asked anxiously as he looked at the stocking dangling from the bed rail.

"Yes, of course he will, dear," said Jane reassuringly. "Now lie down and go to sleep."

She went out of the room, and Michael snuggled into his pillow. He was soon fast asleep, and dreaming that he saw Santa Claus in his reindeer sleigh come galloping down the sky and across the tree-tops in the Merriemead woods; but just as the sleigh drew up

on the roof near the nursery chimney,
Michael woke up.

MICHAEL RAN TO THE WINDOW

The room was flooded with moonlight,
and for some moments he lay staring at the

58

dark shadows cast by the furniture; then the clock in the corridor began to strike.

"Twelve o'clock!" exclaimed Michael; and he looked eagerly towards the stocking; but there were no mysterious bulges in it to indicate a generous filling from Santa Claus's hand. Michael jumped out of bed and ran to the window—not even the faintest tinkle of a sleigh bell came to his listening ear. Santa Claus had forgotten him, after all.

"P'raps he doesn't just know I'm spending Christmas with Grandfather," thought Michael, trying to make every excuse for Santa Claus, but the idea didn't quite make up for that empty stocking hanging so limp and flat on the bed rail, and he pressed his snub nose against the cold window pane, and drearily gazed out at the glittering hoar frost on the trees.

Suddenly a footstep tiptoed along the corridor, and stopped outside the nursery door. Michael held his breath, wondering what would happen next; then the knob turned softly, and in walked a tall figure clad in a long scarlet cloak and a furred cap.

" Ooo—oo! " Michael drew an ecstatic breath. " It's Santa Claus! "

The visitor paused when he saw Michael standing there, and seemed almost inclined to retreat.

" Why didn't you come down the chimney? " asked Michael.

" The chimneys in this old house are too twisty for me to travel down," Santa Claus mumbled into his beard; and he began to thrust various small packets into the stocking, while Michael stood beside him, wide-eyed with excitement.

But Michael was not the only onlooker at this thrilling ceremony. Tatters was peacefully snoring away the night in a happy dream world where bones, biscuits, Slinker and Cook played a large part, especially Cook, when something cold was thrust into his ear. Tatters woke with a jerk.

"G'rrrr!" he growled, just to show the cold 'something' that he wasn't afraid; but it proved to be nothing more formidable than the moist nose of brother Rags who, in an excited whisper, was urging Tatters to "wake up, quick!"

"Wha'smatter?" yawned Tatters sleepily.

"Hush! There's something happening in Michael's room—look!"

The door leading from the day nursery into Michael's bedroom was wide open, and through it Tatters saw the scarlet clad figure of Santa Claus, for a moment he gazed in silence; then—

"Rags," he asked in a puzzled tone, "do old gentlemen with long white beards *always* pack their parcels into stockings?"

"Don't know." Rags was also puzzled. "We'll ask Slinker when we go home—he knows everything. You see, Slinker is the kind of dog that——" Rags stopped, he had just noticed the toys which Santa Claus was carrying under his cloak. "I think it's a burglar, Tatters," he whispered anxiously. "He's stealing Michael's toys."

"Shall we bite him?"

"Yes—come on!"

"Get away, you little rascals!" cried Santa Claus as they both leapt at him.

"Hang on to his cloak, Tatters, while I

get my teeth into his ankle!" gurgled Rags ferociously.

Santa Claus stooped to drive them off, and his long white beard came within reach

RAGS WAS ALSO PUZZLED

of their eager jaws. Rags made a snap, and the beard and fur cap came off, revealing to Michael's astonished eyes the familiar features of Mr. Timson, the butler.

" Ahem! I'm afraid, Master Michael, I've somewhat disturbed your night's rest," began Mr. Timson in his most dignified tone; then he began to laugh, and Michael joined in.

By this time the puppies' yelps had roused the household, and Grandfather entered the room, followed by Jane and the servants.

Bill and Binks, whose sleeping quarters were downstairs, had also heard the uproar, and realising at once that the household was urgently in need of their united protection, they charged wildly up and down the corridors, sending out a duet of challenging barks.

" Burglars . . . in the study! " panted Binks.

They swept into the study, only to find it empty.

" No; they're in the dining-room! " gasped Bill; but the dining-room was also empty.

Rags was still triumphantly gripping the white beard

" Upstairs! " ordered Binks.

The couple of sleuths raced up the broad staircase and along more corridors until, in rounding a dark corner, something soft and hairy rammed them.

" G'rrrr! " rumbled Binks savagely. " I've caught him, Bill! "

But Bill had already sensed the identity of that small hairy body, and pinning it firmly against the wall with his nose, he demanded to know what Rags meant by disturbing the household at that time of night.

Rags was still triumphantly gripping the white beard and cap belonging to Santa Claus, but at Bill's question, he dropped his booty and explained.

" Great bones! " cried the shocked Binks. " You did all that to my Mister Timson? "

" Yes," boasted Rags. " I bit a norful

65

c

big chunk out of his ankle, and——"

But the thrilling account of what Rags had done to Binks's Mister Timson came to an untimely end as Bill took the impudent puppy

"YOU DID ALL THAT TO MY MISTER TIMSON?"

by the scruff of his neck and gave him a good shaking just to teach him manners.

Meanwhile, the servants were clustered round the door of the night nursery, asking what the disturbance was about.

" Has anything happened to the poor lamb? " asked Cook, looking anxiously at Michael.

Tatters thought Cook meant himself, and seeing her red face peering over Jane's shoulder, he sat up and begged, just on the chance she had brought a tasty " something " to bestow on him.

" It's all right—nobody's hurt," said Grandfather reassuringly; and the servants went away, accompanied by Mr. Timson in his scarlet cloak.

" Grandfather," whispered Michael, when they had gone, " didn't Mr. Timson look funny after——"

" After Rags and Tatters had finished with him—eh? "

" Yes." Michael bubbled with laughter.

" But I'm not sure that they don't deserve a good whipping," chuckled Grandfather,

" because you weren't supposed to know that it *was* Timson."

" Why did he do it? " asked Michael.

" Well, Micky boy, it's such a very long time since Santa Claus visited this old house that I was afraid he might have forgotten the way here, so when it got to twelve o'clock and still he hadn't turned up, Timson and I hatched a little plot."

" And he dressed up as Santa Claus and came to fill my stocking? " Michael added delightedly.

Grandfather nodded.

" But where did he get that jolly scarlet cloak? " asked Michael curiously. " He doesn't always wear it."

" Well, no," laughed Grandfather. " I borrowed it from the village school; the children are having a gorgeous Christmas tree next week, and Father Christmas is going to distribute the gifts—at least he will if that couple of rascals haven't completely chewed up his beard and cap," and Grand-father looked through the open door at Rags and Tatters who had hurriedly returned to their basket, and were pretending to be fast asleep.

But from beneath Rags' fat little body there peeped out a wisp of white beard and half the fur cap which had recently adorned the dignified head of Mr. Timson.

V

RAGS TO THE RESCUE

ONE morning Rags realised that he was in dire disgrace. The sensation was by no means new to him, but usually he halved the blame with brother Tatters; this morning, however, he had to bear it alone. At first, nobody knew who was the real culprit; all that the household did know was that the two puppies had been found lying asleep on a couch in the drawing-room, and beside them one of the silk cushions was torn to shreds, with its feathers flying about the room.

In the afternoon, however, the culprit was unexpectedly discovered. A heavy snowstorm

came on, and for some minutes Rags and
Tatters watched the snowflakes whirling past
the window; then suddenly Rags crawled
away under the table and sat with drooping
ears.

" Hello, Rags, what's the matter? " asked
Bill, nosing him out. " Been eating too many
mince pies? "

" No," whimpered Rags. " It's those
dreadful feathers—they're flying about all
over the sky now! I didn't know there were
millions and billions of them in that horrid
cushion when I just nipped——" He stopped
abruptly.

" Oh, so it was *your* fault, after all? "
said Bill.

" Please, Bill, don't tell Binks," pleaded
Rags.

" Don't tell Binks what? " asked a voice,

71

and Binks himself pattered up to see what
the conversation was about.

Rags confessed.

"What—did you tear my silk cushion!"
growled Binks
threateningly.

"Please, Binkie
—I mean, Mister
Binks, I didn't

"IT'S THOSE DREADFUL FEATHERS," WHIMPERED RAGS

72

know it was your cushion, I thought it only belonged to Grandfather."

"Grandfather shares everything with me," replied Binks in a lofty tone. "Yes, even the silk cushions in the drawing-room."

"But, Mister Binks, I really didn't know the feathers would go whirling about all over the sky," wailed Rags, who was feeling dreadfully responsible for the grey gloom outside the window.

"Pooh! Those aren't feathers, they're snowflakes," retorted Binks. "Do you mean to say you don't know what a snowflake is?"

Rags meekly admitted that he hadn't lived long enough to have encountered a snowflake; and in his amazement at such shocking ignorance, Binks quite forgot the outrage on the silk cushion, and explained to both Rags and Tatters exactly what a snowflake was.

All day long the snow fell, and the next morning Merriemead was surrounded by a white world. Tim Stubbs helped Michael to make a snow-man, with two bits of coal for eyes, and a piece of wood for a pipe; and when they crowned their handiwork with a battered old hat, Bill and Binks challenged it with ferocious barks.

Rags and Tatters, who had called in at the kitchen to say good-morning to Cook, missed the first part of the fun, and only arrived in time to see the battered old hat knocked off by a well-aimed snowball from Michael's hand. The dogs immediately pounced on it, and had a right royal battle for possession, in which Binks came off victor with the whole of the brim, leaving what remained of the hat to be divided between his three guests.

74

" I've made 'ee a lovely slide all along the kitchen garden path, Master Michael," said Tim, when the fun was over. " Would 'ee like to come an' try it? "

Of course Michael knew that the very best slides are always made along the kitchen garden path; and he went off eagerly to try the one that Tim Stubbs had made for him.

THE DOGS IMMEDIATELY POUNCED UPON IT

75

Binks didn't think much of slides, so he took his own particular pals a long chase through the orchard and into the spinney where the snow had gathered into drifts.

" I'm thirsty! " Rags stopped, and hung out a quivering tongue.

" So am I," panted Tatters. " Let's go to the pond and get a drink."

" Wait a minute," said Bill. " Where's Binks? "

Binks had suddenly disappeared, leaving not even the print of his paws on the snow-covered ground.

" P'raps he's gone back home," replied Rags. " He told us he always takes Grandfather for a walk in the morning."

Bill accepted the explanation, but still looked about him rather anxiously as he followed the puppies to the pond, for Binks' departure had been amazingly rapid.

" Ooo-oo! " shouted Tatters. " The pond's turned into a big glass window! "

HIS BACK LEGS SUDDENLY SHOT FORWARD

" That's not glass, it's ice," Bill told them; and they scampered on to the frozen surface.

" That's queer," muttered Tatters, when

his back legs suddenly shot forward. " I didn't tell my legs to sit down."

" Very queer! " echoed Rags, finding himself in exactly the same fix. " Never knew my legs to behave in this way before."

He sprang up, took a hurried trot, spread-eagled, and came down with a bang on to his nose.

" If only we h-hadn't t-to manage f-four legs all at o-once it wouldn't be so b-bad! " Tatters jerked out.

" Yes; it's the fault of the back ones; they keep wanting to . . . wough! " Rags spun round and landed on his back.

The next moment there was a soft slither, another fat little body bounced against his, and brother Tatters was also flat on his back gazing upwards.

" Doesn't the sky look funny this way up, Tatters? " remarked Rags, trying to pretend that he was feeling quite happy.

There was silence for a moment; then, " Do you think Slinker could do all that with his legs? " shivered Tatters.

" Yes, of course, he could! " came the emphatic reply. " Slinker's ever so clever! "

Tatters gave a sigh of relief—he was so glad to know that it was only cleverness that had turned the sky upside down, and made his legs do such amazing things.

" Something feels awful cold down my front," began Rags, thinking that a little conversation might cheer matters up a bit. " No, I don't mean my front—that's turned round now—I mean——" Rags waved a feeble paw and tried to decide just what he did mean.

"You little silly!" snuffled a gruff voice in his ear. "If you lie here any longer you'll be frozen stiff!" and Bill's bristly muzzle pushed Rags across the ice until he got him on to the bank, then Tatters was retrieved in the same way.

"Where's Binks?" asked Grandfather, when they all went home. "Has he been with you, Michael?"

"No, Grandfather," replied Michael. "He went off with Bill and the puppies."

Shouts of "Binks!" echoed through the house, but there was no response.

"We must search for him," said Grandfather, looking dreadfully anxious; "he'll freeze to death if he's lost in one of the drifts."

So a search party set off and scoured the fields and woods shouting, "Binks!

Bin-n-n-ks!" but still there was no sign of the truant.

"Come on, Tatters—*we'll* find him!" cried Rags, and they raced off to the spinney.

"We were standing just here when we first missed him," said Tatters.

"Yes." Rags gazed about for a moment, then began to patter up and down, snuffing excitedly at the ground in the way he had seen Bill try to find bones and other important things that were lost. Tatters also snuffed and pattered, but it didn't seem to bring them any nearer to the lost Binks.

"P'raps you don't smell for Binks in the same way as you smell for bones," said Tatters at last.

Rags drearily agreed, and was turning away from the spot when two little black tufts, sticking up out of a mound of snow, attracted his attention. He cocked an enquiring ear, then flung himself on the mound and started a frantic scratching.

"IT'S BINKS!" HE YELPED JOYOUSLY

" It's Binks! " he yelped joyously. " These are his ears! "

" I'll soon get him out," cried Bill, racing up at this moment; and his great paws quickly

82

scattered the snow and released poor Binks, who had fallen into a snowdrift and was too frozen to scratch his way out.

" Oh, Binkie, old bun——" began Rags, joyously disrespectful. " I mean, *Mister* Binkie, old bun, I am so glad you're safe! "

" It was Rags who found you," broke in Tatters. " He saw your ears sticking up."

Binks looked at Rags. " You may drop the ' Mister ' before my name," he said graciously, " and I don't mind if you put ' old bun ' after it, either."

Later on that same day Binks bestowed even a greater favour on his rescuer—he gave him permission to sleep on the silk cushions in the drawing-room!

VI

THE snow lay thick on the roads, and Michael's return to town was delayed for a whole week. Rags and Tatters were dreadfully anxious about Slinker, and they talked of running back home by themselves just to see if he was all right.

" He'll have finished all those biscuits by this time," they told Bill.

" Yes; but you know we left him that nice mouldy bone as well," said Bill consolingly.

But Binks, who was consulted on the matter, gave it as his opinion that bones,

even nice ripe ones, were not very sustaining
for a dog like Slinker; and Rags and Tatters
were plunged into fresh gloom.

However, the snow began to melt at last,

BINKS WAS CONSULTED ON THE MATTER

and Daddy came to take Michael home.
Rags and Tatters took a regretful farewell
of Cook, Bill raced down to the potting-shed
to say good-bye to Tim Stubbs, and the
whole household assembled at the front

85

door to speed the " little master " on his journey.

" Good-bye, Grandfather! " cried Michael. " May I bring Bill and the puppies when I come again? "

" Of course you may, Micky boy," replied Grandfather. " Binks will give them a good welcome."

" Where *is* Binks? " asked Michael. " I haven't said good-bye to him yet."

" It's strange he isn't here," said Grandfather.

It certainly was strange, for no visitor to Merriemead ever arrived without Binks being on the spot to see that the welcome was sufficiently warm, or departed without him being there to see that the send off was sufficiently speedy.

Rags cast an anxious eye across the garden,

but the snow had nearly all melted now; and even the snow-man had dwindled away until there was not enough of him left to have hidden Binks.

" I suppose you didn't pack him in that big bag by mistake, Jane? " laughed Grandfather.

Mr. Timson, who was standing near, permitted his dignified features to relax into a smile, and answered for Jane.

" No, sir, he can't be inside Master Michael's luggage because I saw him carrying his stick across the hall only ten minutes since."

" H'm, well," said Grandfather, " it's shocking bad manners of him not to be here, but I'm sure you'll forgive him, Micky— I'm afraid I spoil the little rascal."

So the car started off with Michael sitting beside Daddy at the wheel, and the three dogs behind with Jane.

" I'm s'prised at Binks," said Rags, in a shocked tone. The puppies were lying on the seat beside an extra travelling rug that had been brought in case Michael felt very cold and needed two.

" Yes, if *I'd* made other pups call me ' Mister ', I'd have been polite enough to come and say good-bye to them." Tatters gave a superior sniff.

" P'raps he had to go down to his rat hole," said Bill, loyally defending the absent Binks. " When the rats come rushing out all together, Binks has to get awful busy to catch them."

" Pooh! " scoffed Tatters. " I don't believe Binks has ever caught a real rat in all his

TATTERS GAVE A
SUPERIOR SNIFF life."

88

" Oh, hasn't he! " came an indignant whisper close to Tatters' ear, and a black nose was thrust out of the folds of the travelling rug.

" Binks! " gasped Tatters.

" Hush! " Binks' nose disappeared, but from beneath the rug came a muffled explanation. " I wanted to go back with you so that I could see Slinker, and I hid under this rug when I heard Jane say it was just an extra one, and might not be needed on the journey."

" Ooo-oo—how jolly! " cried Rags delightedly.

" Don't speak too loud, else Jane'll wonder what's the matter," whispered Binks warningly.

" She's not listening—something went wrong with her knitting when the car joggled,

89

and now she's frowning at it." Rags passed
this bit of news to the stowaway under the rug.

But Daddy had heard the soft whimpers

A BLACK NOSE WAS THRUST OUT

in which the conversation had been carried
on, and he looked over his shoulder.

"What's the matter with those two
puppies, Jane?" he asked. "Better wrap
them up in that rug—they may feel cold."

Jane put out her hand to lift up the rug, then dropped it with a shriek.

"What's happened?" asked Daddy anxiously; and he brought the car to a standstill with a jerk.

"Something cold touched my hand," gasped Jane. "Something inside the rug."

"P'raps it's a toad or—or—a snake!" cried Michael, rather hoping that it might be something really exciting.

Jane flung open the door of the car and stood in the road, holding her skirts very tightly round her ankles in case it was a toad, and Daddy investigated the mystery of the rug.

"Go away!" yapped Rags, anxious lest Binks should be discovered and sent home.

But Daddy brushed aside the valiant defender and lifted up the rug.

"Binks!" he exclaimed in dismay.

" Oh, Daddy, can we take him to London with us? " Michael asked eagerly.

" I'm afraid we must," replied Daddy, looking rather worried. " We're too far on our journey to turn back now, but I'll take him down to Merriemead next week."

" Won't Grandfather be dreadfully unhappy if he thinks Binks is really lost? " said Michael.

" Yes, so we'll send him a message as soon as possible to say that the truant is with us."

The car sped on its way again, and Rags, Tatters and Bill told Binks about all the wonderful things they would show him in London Town.

" I've brought my stick with me, and I would have brought my rat hole as well, to give to Slinker, only "—Binks hesitated— " only I couldn't pack it very well."

" Quite so," replied Bill, who thoroughly

understood the difficulty of carrying about one's own private rat hole; and he tactfully assured their prospective guest that Michael's

RAGS BOLTED IN FIRST OF ALL

house contained most superior rat holes, and one should be placed at Binks' service immediately they arrived.

When the journey ended, and Michael's

93

big front door opened to admit the travellers, Rags bolted in first of all.

" Come on! " he cried, and the others streaked after him up the stairs to Slinker's kennel.

The biscuits and the bone had vanished, and even the cushion was not there.

" Oh, poor Slinker! " wailed Rags. " He must have been starving! "

" Yes," whimpered Tatters, " because he's eaten our cushion as well! "

But later in the evening, when they found the cushion in its usual place in their basket, the couple felt more hopeful about Slinker's fate.

The next morning, a pale wintry sun shone out, and Jane said Michael could go for a walk.

" Now where are those two tiresome puppies? " she asked, when Michael was buttoned into his coat and ready to start.

To Slinker's Rescue

Nobody knew, but away at the top of the house could be heard an excited yapping. Jane went up to see about it, taking with her

MISTER BINKS WAS DREADFULLY 'TELLIGENT

the puppies' leash and a very severe expression.

" Bless me, now what do you want in

95

there?" she cried, finding Bill and Binks wildly scratching at the box room door, while Rags and Tatters urged them on with encouraging yaps.

She opened the door and there was a united rush to get inside; but the room was empty. For a moment Rags looked crestfallen; then he turned round very quickly.

"There he is . . . there's Slinker!"

Yes, there was the grey dog standing flat against the wall, just as Rags had seen him on that first day; but strange to say there were now three more Slinkers standing beside him.

"Why, Slinker is nothing but your own shadow, after all!" cried Binks. "Look, it's the sun shining through the window that makes it—we're all there."

Yes — Mister Binks was *dreadfully* 'telligent!

PRINTED FOR THE PUBLISHERS
BY W. & J. MACKAY & CO., LTD., CHATHAM
547/953
6401